B·U·G·
Be You Guardians
Time to be yourself

Meet the BUGs!

Little bugs with big hearts, the BU Guardians (BUGs) are there to help whenever they are needed. With a friendly ear or a few kind words, the BU Guardians help friends to stand tall and be the best version of themselves. After all, being YOU is the very best thing you can do!

In the stories in this series, each friendly and supportive BUG has a special skill.

Can you spot **Bruno** on each page?

Freddie

Shines a light on others' talents.

Sia

Knows that it's OK to make mistakes.

Chester

Teaches that it's good to ask for help.

Coco

Reminds others of their strengths.

Luna

Celebrates divers and uniqueness

Bruno

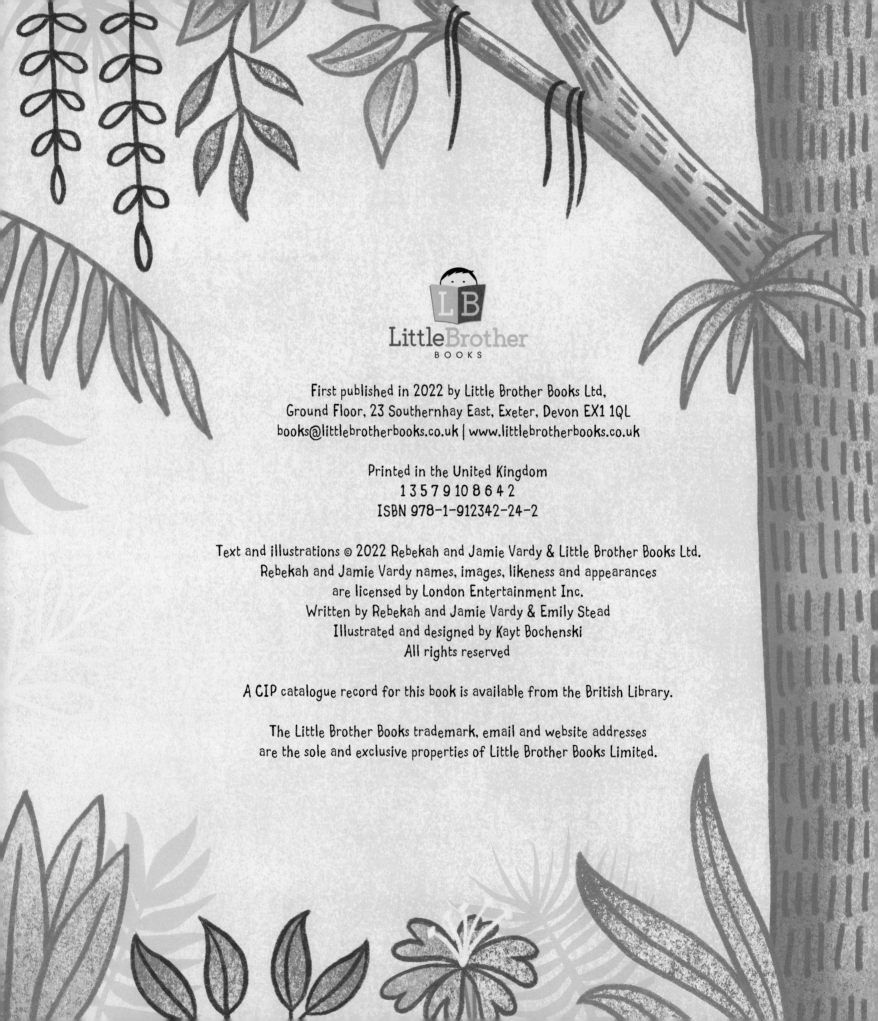

LittleBrother
BOOKS

First published in 2022 by Little Brother Books Ltd,
Ground Floor, 23 Southernhay East, Exeter, Devon EX1 1QL
books@littlebrotherbooks.co.uk | www.littlebrotherbooks.co.uk

Printed in the United Kingdom
1 3 5 7 9 10 8 6 4 2
ISBN 978-1-912342-24-2

Text and illustrations © 2022 Rebekah and Jamie Vardy & Little Brother Books Ltd.
Rebekah and Jamie Vardy names, images, likeness and appearances
are licensed by London Entertainment Inc.
Written by Rebekah and Jamie Vardy & Emily Stead
Illustrated and designed by Kayt Bochenski

A CIP catalogue record for this book is available from the British Library.

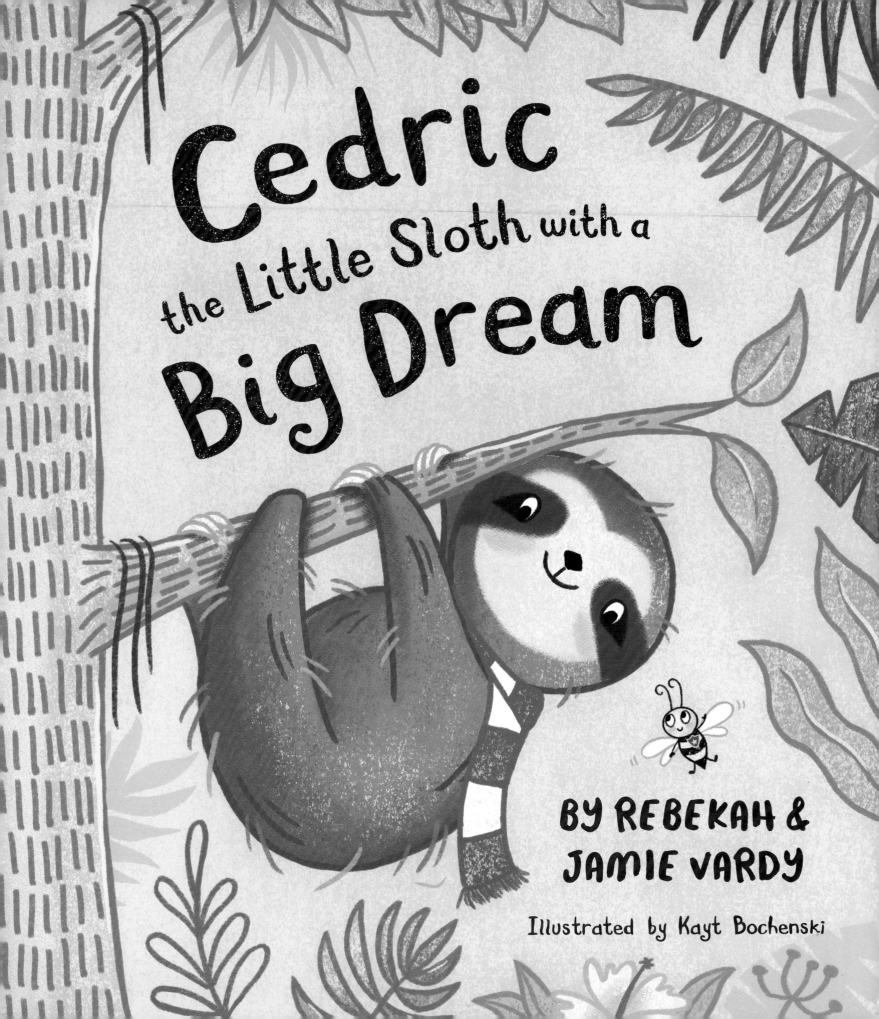

Cedric
the Little Sloth with a
Big Dream

BY REBEKAH & JAMIE VARDY

Illustrated by Kayt Bochenski

Deep in the jungle a football team played,
thrilling and **dazzling**
with every display.

Whether feathered or furry,
they played like a **dream**,

Rainforest Rovers, the name of their team.

Cedric the sloth was the club's biggest fan.
He clapped and he cheered
when each match began.

Then one day he plucked
up the courage to say,

"Excuse me, but sometime, could I maybe play?"

"A sloth on the team? Don't make me laugh," growled Tiger, who chipped a high ball to Giraffe.

"You're too slow and sleepy to be on our side,"

the lemur twins giggled, and Cedric just sighed.

So off sloped the sloth feeling terribly sad.
"I wish I could play," Cedric cried to his dad.

"Oh, Cedric! I'm sorry," Dad replied, trying to rest.
"But sleeping – not football's – the thing we do best."

That night in the trees, while others were snoring,
Cedric, still wide awake, was dreaming of scoring.

GOAL!

As the sun in the morning rose orange and pink, the sloth hadn't slept, not one single wink.

Next morning the team had their **biggest** match yet,

a final the Rovers would **never** forget.

If they tried their best
and **never** gave up,

the top prize could be theirs –
the famed **Jungle Cup!**

A quick ball from kick-off reached Toucan who **soared** to tap in with his beak –

the first goal had been scored!

Cedric danced up and down, cheering,
"Hip, hip, hooray!"

The game looked such fun,
how he wished he could play!

The scores were soon tied
thanks to Snake's **sneaky** goal.

She slid for the ball,
and then **swallowed it whole!**

No one could stop her,
as Snake crossed the line.

"Eating? That's cheating!" Cedric shrieked from his vine.

Tiger struck next with his **fearsome** left paw.

"**2-1! 2-1!**" squawked a helpful macaw.

The teams carried on,
with the match almost over,

was the cup set to go to
the Rainforest Rovers?

Disaster then struck with just seconds to go.
The goalie was tripped and injured her toe!

The team captain called out
for the sub to come on,

but quickly discovered

Chameleon gone!

YAWN!

Tiger said sadly, "We can't play with four.
A goal with no keeper? They'll easily score!"

Then in buzzed a BUG with a plan that was good.
The bee couldn't play but knew someone who could!

In the sleepy sloth's ear,
the little BUG cried,

"Don't fall asleep, Cedric!
Please, open your eyes!"

But Cedric **snoozed** on, and had started to **snore**,
exhausted from staying up all night before.

Time for Plan Bee,
the BUG had to think fast,

TEE HEE!

so he **tickled**
the sloth,

who woke up
at last.

"Your team needs you, Cedric, it's time to step up.
You've got this," he smiled. "Now go help win the cup!"

Then on to the pitch strolled the
**super
sloth sub,**
to play his first match
for his **favourite** club.

With each shot on goal

Cedric stretched like elastic.

He sent the crowd **wild.**

He was simply **fantastic!**

"You're number one, Cedric!"
said his teammates, delighted,

and Cedric just smiled,
feeling proud and excited.

The whistle blew loudly – the match was now over.
The winners, of course, were the
Rainforest Rovers!

So remember, no matter how hard it may seem, like Cedric, don't ever give up on your dream.

You're special, fantastic, just as you are, so always B U – and you'll be a **star**.

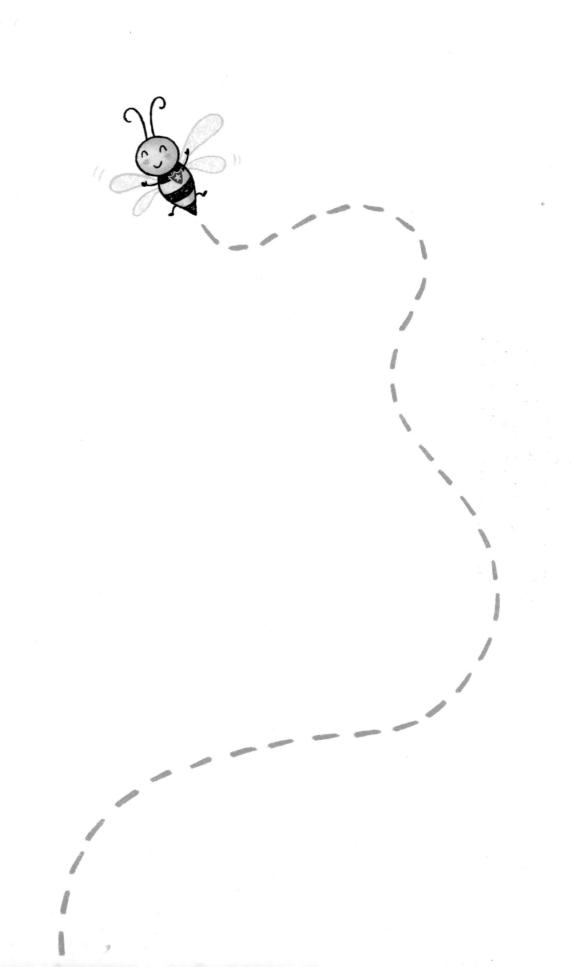